For Peggy and
Tom Bender

The moon had just risen high over the hill.
The stars were all out. It was quiet and still.
But instead of the sound of snoring and sleeping,
Jillian Jiggs heard somebody weeping.

"I'm scared of the monster," said her little sister. Jillian held her and Jillian kissed her.

3

"It's okay, Rebecca. Get into my bed.
I'll chase that bad monster right out of your head.
And then in the morning, you know what we'll do?
We'll show that bad monster that he can't scare you."

And this is what happened the very next day,
When Rachel and Peter came over to play.

"Hi, Rachel! Hi, Peter! Quick, get inside.
The monster might catch you," Jillian cried.
"He's scaring Rebecca. He's mangy. He's MEAN!
To stop him we're making...

7

...a MONSTER MACHINE!
This monster machine will shrink him so small,
He'll be squished. He'll be squashed.
He'll be nothing at all."

"We'll help," Peter said. "Four is better than two.
You never can tell what a monster might do."

9

They worked the whole morning and when they were done,
Jillian warned them, "This won't be all fun.
Remember the magic word: KALAMAZOO.
It makes you strong, and monster-proof, too.
That mangy, mean monster can't scare us, you know.
Are you ready, Rebecca? Come on now. Let's go!"

"Kalamazoo! Kalamazoo!
Monster, you're meatloaf! Monster, you're through!

Our monster machine will shrink you so small,
You'll be squished. You'll be squashed.
You'll be nothing at all."

They had to be sneaky and circle around,
Looking for clues that lay deep underground.

They followed the tracks. They were fearless and steady.
They never gave up. They were rough, tough and ready.

"Kalamazoo! Kalamazoo!
Monster, you're meatloaf. Monster, you're through!

Our monster machine will shrink you so small,
You'll be squished. You'll be squashed.
You'll be nothing at all."

The monster was clever, he kept out of sight.
He knew he'd be stronger much later...at night!
But deep in the forest, the road turned and dipped,

And he wasn't careful. He stumbled and tripped.
"Shh!" said Rebecca. "Did you hear that thumping?
Look over there, the bushes are bumping."

"It's him. It's the monster. He's lurking in there,"
Said Jillian Jiggs. "Better BEWARE!"

"Oh, no!" said Rebecca. "Remember, he's mean!
This looks like a job for the monster machine!"

They filled a big pot with some green grass and dirt
And smushed it together for monster dessert!

The pot was then left by the monster machine
And all of them hid where they couldn't be seen.

"Get down," said Rebecca. "The monster's awake."

The monster came nearer. They felt the ground shake.
Nearer and nearer until...

...the box SNAPPED!
"Aha!" said Rebecca. "Monster, you're trapped!"

"Kalamazoo! Kalamazoo!
Monster, you're meatloaf. Monster, you're through!
Our monster machine will shrink you so small,
You'll be squished. You'll be squashed.
You'll be nothing at all."

They switched the great switch on the monster machine.
"We'll squish-squash him down to the size of a bean!"
The clickers were clicking. The lights started blinking.

"Yes!" said Rebecca. "The monster is shrinking."

"Monster, O Monster, why are you mean?
Why do you roar and shout in her dream?
Monster, O Monster, why are you bad?"

"I think," said Rebecca, "I think that he's sad.
He might have been lonely, he needs friends like you.
He might have been angry and that's why he grew."

"We'd better shrink him a little bit more,
Then he won't scare you like he did before."

"Stop!" said Rebecca. "Enough is enough."

They didn't listen, they kept acting tough.
They didn't listen. They kept right on going,
The squishing and squashing showed no sign of slowing.
Then the monster machine began bumping about.

"Look," said Rebecca, "he wants to get out! Can't we be friends? Can't he play too?"

The monster agreed. The monster said...